A note for parents and teachers . . .

Shape Rhymes introduces basic two-dimensional shapes. The poems present simple instructions that define the shapes, and the pictures illustrate examples of the shape or shapes described. After the shapes are introduced, the poems ask the child to find examples in the pictures. When helpful, additional familiar examples are drawn from the child's own world and experience.

Shape Rhymes

1   2   3   4   5   6   7   8   9   0   89   88   87   86   85

ISBN 0-8172-2444-0 lib. bdg.

ISBN 0-8172-2449-1 softcover

Shape Rhymes

Written by
Jan Gleiter

Illustrated by
Chrissie Wells

Raintree Childrens Books
Milwaukee • Toronto • Melbourne • London

The teacher is teaching these nice little bears
About different shapes, like circles and squares.
A square has four sides, and each side is the same.
How many square things in this room can you
    name?

There are squares on the floor. There are really a
    lot!
Some more things are square, and others are not.
The bears can find squares, and they think it is
    fun.
One picture is square. Now, do you know which
    one?

These bears are outside. They are having a talk
About how many round things they see on their
    walk.
The doorbell is round, and so is the sun.
The bears think that looking for round things is
    fun.

Just look now at all of the wheels on the cars.
Can you see all the other round things that there
    are?
A round thing that's flat is a circle, you know.
Like the sign on the post that tells cars where to go.

Look at the paper the teacher has got.
Is that shape a square or a circle? It's not!
That shape's called a triangle. Look and you'll see.
How many sides does it have? That's right, three!

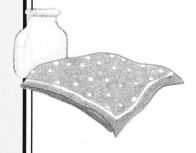

There are triangles up on the wall. They are red.
And somebody has one that's tied on her head.
There's one more another bear's showing to you.
It, too, has three sides, as all triangles do.

The teacher says, "Children, now look here at me.
This book is a rectangle shape. Can you see?
It's a lot like a square. Do you see the four sides?
But a rectangle's taller, see, than it is wide.

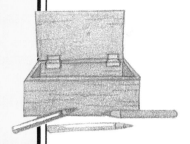

"Or sometimes it's wider than it is tall.
Can you see one like that right up there on the wall?
Lots of boxes are rectangles. So is a bed.
And so are most all of the books you have read."

These little bears are as good as can be
While they look at some pictures they wanted to see.
The big bear's an artist. He painted them all.
He made every picture you see on the wall.

Some pictures are big, and some pictures are small.
Some pictures are wide, and some pictures are tall.
But most of the pictures are all shaped the same.
What do you call them? Rectangle's the name.

These bears are all trying to pick and to choose
The wallpaper that's the best paper to use.
Each one likes a certain shape more than the rest.
Each one thinks a different design is the best.

There are rectangles, triangles, circles, and squares.
Which one is the favorite of each of the bears?
Will they ever choose which one to use? Well,
   they may.
But I think that deciding will take them all day!

The school day is over. The bears want to play.
They run to the park. It is not a long way.
One bear likes to rest while he's reading a book.
Do you see that it's square? You will if you look.

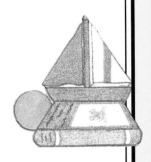

One bounces a ball so high up off the ground.
Two others sail boats on a pond that is round.
The sails on the boats are triangles, you know.
And when the wind blows, you should see the
    boats go!

Two bears are enjoying their playtime together.
It's raining outside. But they don't mind the
  weather.
They play with their blocks. They are making a
  town.
I hope that the buildings they've made don't fall
  down.

Now, making a town is a fun thing to do,
With rectangles, squares, and some triangles, too.
They use lots of shapes in this rainy day game.
How many of them can you point to and name?

There are some shapes that you know in this
    picture of bears.
Do you see something round? Do you see the two
    squares?
But the boat is an oval. Now, that's something new.
If you wait I will try to explain it to you.

If you took a circle and pulled on two sides,
You'd have a shape longer than it was wide.
It would look like an egg or a racetrack, you see.
A shape called an oval is what it would be.

It's winter and snow is all over the ground.
The bears made some snowballs, so white and so
round.
One bear has slipped off a rectangular sled.
She's going to fall, plop, in the snow on her head.

Do you see the one bear who is walking so tall
On top of square boxes? She might trip and fall.
But if she does slip, she'll be up in a minute.
Since snow doesn't hurt bears who trip and land in
it.

Here's a bear with a birthday. Her party's today.
And all of her friends have come over to play.
They're tired from games. So they sit on the floor
And try to find rectangles, circles, and more.

The bears look around while they're all sitting
   down.
There are shapes on the curtains, the pillow, the
   crowns.
What shape is the mirror that's up on the wall?
What shape are the presents? What shape is the
   ball?

This bear is at home. She is staying in bed.
She's got quite a terrible cold in her head.
"I have nothing to do!" the little bear cries.
"Yes, you do," says her mother. "I've got a
   surprise.

"I've brought you a book and some paper and
   glue.
You can cut out some shapes. See how well you
   can do."
She cuts circles, squares, triangles, rectangles,
   look!
Can you find where she's stuck every shape in her
   book?

1. What you read in this book were poems. A poem uses words that rhyme. That means that they sound alike, like *bear* and *square*. See if you can think of words that sound like these:

bed	car
game	door
bake	sail

2. Now see if you can finish these poems. Fill in the blank at the end of each one. The word you choose should sound like the word in capital letters.

Count all the sides of the shapes that you SEE.
Rectangles have four, and triangles have

_____ .

A square is the same length on every SIDE.
It's always as tall, you see, as it is _____ .

A bear who knew shapes said to his little
    BROTHER,
"A rectangle's longer one way than the

_____ .

Things that are circles will roll on the
    GROUND.
That's because circles are always so

_____ .